Advanced Praise for *The Painted Series: The Adventures of Bleecker, and Banjo:*

"A superb collection of impressionistic art depicting the beauty of the Linville Gorge wilderness area by one of our community's friendliest native residents, there is no doubt you are going to enjoy this compilation of images by Tonja."—Chris Garner, TPS Photography – PPA Master Photographer & Photographic Craftsman.

"Join authors Tonja Smith and Emily Smith and their canine companions on this beautifully rendered tour of the natural wonders of Burke County. This book should inspire anyone from six to sixty to venture out and see for themselves the grandeur that awaits in our backyard. Hmm, think I'll go lace up my boots..."—David Benner, co-author of *Carolina Whitewater*.

"I loved how the pictures looked really realistic. I loved how curious the pups were, and I like their names".—Loretta Jones, age 7.

"I like how the pups got to see the river and play in the river. And I love how they were on the tippy top and got to see the water."—Lacey Jones, age 4.

The Painted Series

The Adventures of

Bailey, Bleecker, and Banjo

Linville Gorge

Story by Emily and Tonja Smith
Illustrations by Tonja Smith

REDHAWK
PUBLICATIONS

Heres to many great
adventures!

Emily S.
Tonja Smith

Redhawk Publications
2550 US Hwy 70 SE
Hickory, NC 28602

ISBN: 978-1-952485-32-9

Robert Canipe, General Editor.
Patty Thompson, Project Manager, Permissions
Coordinator, and Fan Club Poobah.

In Memory of Bailey:
Life with you was filled
with the greatest of adventures.

Special Note

In this book, the fictional Painted Adventures of Bailey, Bleecker, and Banjo take place in Burke County, North Carolina. This is the un-ceded land of the Cherokee and Catawba Tribes. Many of the sites are within the Linville Gorge, or *Eeseeoh*, the Cherokee word meaning "River of Cliffs."

We acknowledge and honor these tribes for the stewardship of the land, past, present, and future in their traditional territories.

Credit to Eli Smith.

Acknowledgements

A special thank you to my son Eli Smith for sharing photographs and information from his Gorge adventures.

Many thanks to Lora Whitener, Kit Jones, Morgan Hodson, Angela Shores, Ph.D. and Adventure Bound Books, Leslie Cothern, David Benner, Mark D. Phillips, and Sahil Patel.

Most importantly, thank you to my husband Wayne Smith and Bailey, Bleecker, Banjo, and Caroline.

Foreword

Follow Bailey, Bleecker and Banjo as they explore "Nature's Playground" in Burke County, in the foothills and mountains of western North Carolina. Thousands of human visitors bring their furry friends to Burke every year as they seek new adventures in the state parks, national forests and other attractions. Many visitors choose to camp under the stars near Table Rock and the Linville Gorge, while others enjoy more modern accommodations in pet-friendly hotels and vacation rentals.

The artwork found in this book are all real places in Burke County. I hope you will come visit!

Ed Phillips
Burke County Tourism Development Authority
www.discoverburkecounty.com

Chapter One

Bailey, Bleecker, and Banjo lived with their family by the banks of Moss Creek. Bailey, the black and white sheepdog, was a wise and gentle soul who always seemed to be smiling. Bleecker, the shepherd, was happiest when she was busy working and learning. Banjo, the rescue, was the youngest and smallest of the three and the last to join the pack. Banjo loved to play and explore. The three spent endless hours romping in the winding creek, sitting around the campfire at night with their friends, and wandering the trails in their great backyard.

Being the oldest, Bailey entranced Bleecker and Banjo with riveting stories of past adventures. She told the younger pups tales of hiking in the big mountains, of splashing in the cold refreshing creeks, and of romping in fields where all she could see was a golden glow from a sea of daffodils.

Bailey shared stories of exploring what was once a charming old dairy farm that had milk cows near a big lake. She told of peeking into abandoned buildings made of stone and running through fields of tall grass. She described being on trails under towering trees and blooming mountain laurels. Bailey had endless fantastic tales that stirred the pups' imaginations.

Always enthralled with Bailey's stories, Bleecker and Banjo pleaded with her to take them on an adventure of their own. From Moss Creek, they could see the big mountains in the distance and they could hear them silently beckoning.

At last, with a beautiful day in their wake, the sweet sheepdog agreed it was time and began leading the trio. With wagging tails, happy dances, and shrill yips they couldn't contain, the journey began!

Chapter Two

Bailey was thrilled to introduce the pups to their first stop, a winding trail through a forest that surrounded a lake. The forest was peaceful and the pups were delighted as they walked across a beautiful bridge and alongside the bikers and hikers. Along the trails, they saw colored, metal leaves on trees that marked the way for humans. Bailey, however, knew the way by heart.

19

The blue sparkling water of the lake beside them was irresistible, and they decided to go for a swim. The little pup spotted a red canoe on the beach that appeared to be waiting just for them! While canoeing, they saw turtles sunbathing on logs, herons fishing on the beaches, and hawks flying high in the sky.

With paws back on dry land, Bailey began leading them up the mountain. Unable to contain their joy, Bleecker and Banjo began charging at full speed. After a long run, Bailey grew weary and spotted an empty hammock. It was as inviting as the canoe had been. The three jumped in, curled up, and took a nap. When they woke, Bailey told them the great mountain in the distance was part of their grand adventure, and they would get to climb its peak tomorrow.

TONJA

23

Chapter Three

Feeling refreshed after their nap and ready to continue, Bailey led the youngsters to the place where she had once seen the most beautiful sunset. The dogs watched in awe as the sky was painted in front of their eyes. Brilliant hues of oranges, yellows, pinks, and purples filled the once-blue canvas and the mountains just beyond them.

Bailey told them about mysterious lights that can be seen in these mountains sometimes ... just sometimes ... if you're lucky. Bleecker and Banjo waited patiently and quietly as night fell. Suddenly, stillness faded as orbs of blue and reddish-orange appeared out of nowhere. The lights put on a spectacular show-dancing, bouncing, multiplying, and floating! The pups were disappointed when the lights disappeared from the sky and wanted an encore. The performance was over much too soon!

After seeing the magic of the lights, the canine companions trekked on the moonlit trail. As mysteriously as the red canoe and the red hammock had appeared earlier, they came upon a red tent with a crackling campfire. The stars danced above the treetops as the three pups began to yawn, feeling tired from their first day of adventure. Bailey kept her watchful sheepdog eye trained on the tent opening. As the last flicker of fire went out, Bleecker and Banjo hushed their whispers and fell fast asleep.

Chapter Four

Morning broke and the second day of the greatest adventure for Bailey, Bleecker, and Banjo continued on the trail by their campsite. Not long into their walk, they heard the thundering music of the mighty river far below that cleaved the mountains. Bleecker and Banjo took a few more moments to gaze down, then dashed to catch the leader of their pack.

Bleecker and Banjo were quite surprised when they came upon a little log cabin, deep in the forest. They took a peek inside where they spied lots of maps, camping gear, and hikers. Bailey's keen instinct and knowledge were all they needed, so back on the trail they went.

33

They could hear the sounds of water roaring throughout the forest. The trail led the trio up, up, up until they saw huge waterfalls and a deep pool of water below them. They wanted to get closer, so Bailey led them around the trails to sit near the top of the colossal rocks where the waterfall provided a cooling mist. After a few refreshing laps of cold mountain water, they were anxious to move on.

The trail took them up a steep slope towards the peak of the mountain. Along the way, they stepped on wiggly rocks and jumped over giant roots. Anxiously, Banjo would ask "Are we there yet?" Bailey tilted her head and smiled and reminded her to always enjoy the journey, it's not just about the destination. Then she led them up the final incline of the trail and at last they reached the mountain peak. The three gingerly ventured out on the huge rocks. They felt as though they were on top of the world!

The pups were curious to explore more of the magnificent mountain top. On the other side, they could also see for miles and miles and miles. Mountains, water, and cities were all below them! Bailey told Bleecker and Banjo that the sliver of shiny blue that was beyond the mountains was part of the lake where they canoed yesterday.

39

Chapter Five

After leaving the mountain top, Bailey told them that it was time to make their way down and on to the next mountain, which was the one they had previously seen from the red hammock. While some trails were steep and rocky, others were easier to maneuver. They walked under the tall hardwoods and past groves of mountain laurels.

41

While on their adventure, they loved to play games. The shepherd and the little pup could not resist playing a game of hide and seek. On the trailhead of another mountain before them, they spotted a hollowed tree that was the perfect hiding spot. Of course, they could never fool Bailey who found them quickly!

Reaching their destination, the pups had never seen so many rocks. Bailey taught them a new activity, and they thought rock hopping was great fun. The view was spectacular! Bailey knew they didn't want to leave the rocks, and neither did she, but she also knew they needed to return to their journey. They had one more summit to make.

Chapter Six

Bleecker and Banjo were a bit sad when Bailey told them they had climbed the last mountain of this venture. However, Bailey assured them they would have more explorations to come, cheering up the pups who were already looking forward to their next adventure. They raced to the last peak, and Bleecker was the first to look over the edge.

TONJA

The three travelers played among the rocks above tree tops-high in the sky-happy to be with one another. Once again they could see the lake down below by the trail with colored metal leaves that would guide them back home. With dusty paws and happy hearts, they took one last look, then began to descend the mountain trail.

49

Chapter Seven

After a very long jaunt, three tired friends came to the big old barn on the hill, and they knew they were almost home. They had spent many sunny afternoons playing on these hills and jumping up on big, round bales of hay. From there, they could see the smaller mountains in the south that cast a shadow over Moss Creek. Once again, Bailey led the way, this time to home.

Caroline, the house cat, anxiously waited by the back door for her best friends to return. Bailey smiled and listened as Bleecker and Banjo excitedly shared a few thrilling stories from their adventure with the feline. Once they were too tired to go on, the four made themselves comfortable on their favorite sofa and fell fast asleep together—their dreams filled with waterfalls and mountain tops.

Linville Gorge is a scenic and rugged Wilderness area in the Pisgah National Forest in Western North Carolina. The gorge is sometimes called the Grand Canyon of the East. Trails range from easy to extreme.

Page 11—Moss Creek is home to the dogs in Western North Carolina.

Page 13—Private property of an old homestead at the base of Shortoff Mountain by the Linville River.

Page 15—The old Whippoorwill Dairy Farm is now home to Fonta Flora Brewery in Nebo, North Carolina. It is surrounded by Lake James State Park.

Page 17—View of Table Rock and Hawksbill Mountains.

Page 19—The Fonta Flora State Trail.

Page 21—Lake James.

Page 23—View of Table Rock Mountain.

Page 25—Wiseman's View Scenic Overlook with a view of Table Rock Mountain.

Page 27—Wiseman's View Scenic Overlook with the mysterious Brown Mountain Lights with a view of Table Rock Mountain and Hawksbill Mountain.

All reference photographs are from the photograph collections of Emily Smith, Eli Smith, and Tonja Smith.

Emily Smith grew up exploring Moss Creek and the mountains surrounding Morganton, NC. She currently resides in Raleigh, NC with Banjo and Caroline. Emily's earliest memory is of sitting on her first dog, Zoey, while reading to her. Now, Emily enjoys Banjo's companionship, listening to music on the porch and wandering the Raleigh Greenway, and as she navigates life.

Tonja Smith was born and continues to live in Western North Carolina with her husband Wayne and dog Bleecker. She has two grown children, Emily (co-author) and Eli. As a visual artist, Tonja focuses on covering canvases with acrylic paints and drawing portraits. You can often spot her black shepherd in her paintings. Tonja works as a Medical Laboratory Technician.

Follow us on Instagram @thepaintedseries

Bailey Smiles
2005-2021
Bailey was a Border Collie who was born and raised in
Morganton, NC. Bailey entered the Smith family in 2005 when
she was traded for a pencil drawing of "Bailey," her breeder's
daughter. For over 15 years, Bailey played at Moss Creek
and explored the many trails in Burke County, where she
always led the way. She grew up visiting Emily's schools from
elementary to college, attended basketball and band practices,
always eager to participate. Whether it was hiking, monitoring
the campfires, listening to music, playing frisbee and dress
up, or waiting for her best friend Mollie to go outside to play,
Bailey was always by your side.

Bleecker is half Beligian Malinois and half German Shepherd and does everything with gusto! She loves to fetch, play hide-and-seek, and cool off in the water at Moss Creek. She is always eager to go anywhere with her owner, Tonja. It's an understatement to say Bleecker is a vocal pup: the more excited she gets, the more she has to say.

Banjo Smith was born in Morganton, NC and now resides in Raleigh, NC with her owner, Emily, and her feline sibling, Caroline. Banjo was rescued from Burke County Animal Services in August, 2020, and she instantly knew Emily was her human. She is an Australian Cattle Dog, German Shepherd, Chihuahua, Beagle, Chow Chow + more mix. Her days are filled with long walks, learning tricks, porch hangs, chasing the cat, and spending time with her human and animal friends.

Made in the USA
Columbia, SC
02 August 2022

64080562R00035